# THE DRUMMER BOY

# THE DRUMMER BOY

CYPRIAN EKWENSI

ISBN: 978-1-960611-10-9 - Paperback
eISBN: 978-1-960611-11-6 - eBook

Library of Congress Control Number: 2023908045

Cover Illustration by Nancy Batra

∞This paper meets the requirements of ANSI/NISO Z39.48-1992 (Permanence of Paper)

050323

# 1

# A CROWD AMONG THE GRASS

Madam Bisi had just left the hospital and was making her way towards the foot of the tree where her taxi was parked. She walked slowly, and with that dignity which befits a woman who is happily married and owns a trading store on Balogun Street. She was not thinking, however, of the crockery, bicycles, and tobacco in her store. Her mind was far too full of painful memories of suffering humanity she had only just seen in the wards, especially of her friend Anti. Anti seemed to be in a terrible way, and it would require all the modern medical skill at the doctor's Command to restore net health. Still, Bisi did not despair. She knew little about illnesses and medicines and she could not foretell what might happen to Anti. It was best to hope and pray.

She found her taxi waiting as arranged under a mango tree, but the driver had apparently decided to employ his time in pursuits less boring than sleeping at the wheel and the little girl Shola must also have joined him.

Madam Bisi leaned against the taxi, and in the intervals between sounding the horn and waiting for them, she allowed herself to observe the visitors who now poured out of the hospital in a never-ending stream. They were a mixed lot. Men in gowns, men in felt hats and English-tailored suits. Women in bouses and wrappers, women in high-heeled shoes and gaily coloured frocks. They were all hurrying, jostling, and scrambling to get away. Hurrying. That was perhaps the only thing common to all of them, their excitement and impatience.

Madam looked down the road to see what the rush was all about, but, making out nothing other than a crowd among the grass, she asked one of the high-heeled girls what she was in such a haste to catch.

"There's something there!" said the girl, pointing.

"Where?" asked Bisi.

"There, at the foot of that tree! Can't you see a crowd?"

"I can see a crowd among the grass. But what are they doing?"

"I don't know, Ma."

The girl looked very impatient to be getting along, and Bisi said, "Please, when you get there, kindly look for a man in a white jumper and white trousers. He's my taxi-driver. Tell him to come and take me home. I'm waiting for him."

"Yes, Ma."

And as the girl joined the hurrying stream, Bisi added, "Tell him to bring Shola, too."

But a quarter of an hour later, Madam Bisi decided that she had tested her patience enough. The driver was not forthcoming, and even Shola, who was carrying the food that Anti had refused to eat, was nowhere to be seen.

Madam Bisi went towards that tree where the crowd was gathered. As she approached, her ears were thrilled by the most exciting drumming she had ever heard. The rhythm of the drum made her move quite unconsciously to the beats, and she knew at once that the drummer was good. The instrument was unfamiliar. It was the kind of drum which West Africans call the samba, but which is really a tambourine, a little instrument, flat and circular, with a chain of bells around the rim. The strokes came out in a succession of loud thuds, at times dying down, at times rising to such a pitch that they drowned the voice of the singer. What a rich and tender voice he had. He sang about the rich and the poor, the suffering and the happy. He sang of love and death and good and evil.

Madam Bisi's blood grew warm with feeling. For a moment, she forgot the object of her quest and stood near the crowd, watching them dance. The women had formed themselves into a half-moon and were now advancing gracefully towards the centre. Suddenly—as the rhythm quickened—they crouched low, and, looking "over their shoulders, worked their hips in short, sideways movements.

The soldiers standing in the half-moon cheered, came forward and put coins on the brows of the women. Gracefully neglecting the money which stuck fast to their dark sweaty brows, they wriggled on, until that wild rhythm stopped suddenly.

"Oh!" Groaned everybody. "More!"

They crowded around the foot of the tree, shouting and begging. Somebody began to hand out palm wine to the women, and, as they raised the gourds to their lips, Bisi asked the man next to her,

"What are they dancing for?"

The man looked at her as curiously as if she were a new and interesting object.

"What are they dancing for?" he frowned. "Madam, does anyone know what he is dancing for when Akin is playing his samba?"

"Who's Akin?"

"That's the boy I'm talking about! Madam, are you a stranger here?"

Having got that out of his system, the disgusted man left Bisi and mingled with the crowd. She remembered, angrily, that she still had not found Shola or the taxi-driver and that the time was getting on.

And then all was silent again. That rich, tender voice came out again, at first gently, singing about love. The bells around the drum scarcely jangled, then the singer became more excited, and his voice grew louder, ever louder. He clapped his drum with such force that the crowd went wild.

In the heat of the excitement, someone touched Bisi on her wrapper. It was her little maid, Shola. But Bisi was not looking. She had eyes only for the drummer boy. There he stood at the foot of the tree, tall, with nothing on him save a pair of white pants. The samba was under his left armpit, and he slapped at it firmly with his bare hands. His hips were parted and the sweet voice which came out moved her to the point of tears.

The boy stopped again as abruptly as he had done the first time, and this time Madam Bisi herself felt a pang of sadness surge through her. The taxi-driver had also joined her, but Bisi paid no attention to him. She opened her purse and took out a ten-shilling note. She forced her way through the crowd, and by the time she got as far as the boy, she was panting.

"Akin," she called. "Akin!"

The drummer boy turned round. There was a smile on his face, but his eyes were closed. Madam Bisi pressed the note into his hands.

"Take this, boy, and God bless you."

He smiled again but did not open his eyes. And then it downed suddenly on Bisi that this boy had not merely closed his eyes out of the excitement of the day.

He was blind.

Such an attractive boy, too.

Madam Bisi left at once.

As the taxi carried her home, Bisi saw that face again and again. A sensitive face, with wide nostrils and a very small mouth. The song she had heard kept coming back to her until the very drone of the car seemed to become a part of it. She told herself that this was not the first blind boy she had ever met. Why then, this terrible shock? Why this wave of pity?

"No," murmured Bisi. "It will soon pass away. I'll soon forget him. There's nothing in it, really."

And after a few days, faced again with her own troubles, she soon forgot all about Akin, the blind drummer boy. She had a lot to do. The little shed on Balogun Street, with its display of crockery, biscuits, and cotton, must be made to bring in money. The Market Women's Society must be run, and she had her husband to look after.

About a week later, Bisi went again to see Anti at the hospital, and this time a miracle had happened. Anti was not on her bed. As she entered the Ward, Bisi saw her at the other end telling a story to the patients with a great flourish of her arms and head. Bisi was glad.

"Anti!" she called. "What are you doing there? Is this how patients in this hospital behave?"

Anti turned and smiled. She walked towards Bisi with a lively step, her eyes bright with new-found health.

"You're getting better, I see, Anti."

"Am I? The doctor says he'll discharge me today, I shall be so happy to get home. I've been lying on my back for over six weeks. Oh, I'm so tired."

She went on to tell Bisi all about the other patients and their troubles, and how they wouldn't let her sleep at night.

"See that one with a baby, she was shouting throughout the night. I was afraid."

"What's wrong with her?"

"I don't know."

Anti was wrapped up in recollections of her experiences when a boy came towards them and, passing close to Bisi, placed a bunch of flowers on Anti's table. He smiles and asked Anti how she felt.

"Is it true that you'll be leaving us soon?"

"Yes, Akin. It is true. Don't you want me to leave?"

"No," said the boy. "Stay with us a little longer."

He came close to Anti and took her hand tenderly. Madam Bisi had turned at the mention of the name Akin, and as she studied the face of the boy before her, she found he was no other than the drummer boy who had thrilled a whole crowd with his little tambourine or samba. He was now dressed in a blue jumper which came down to his knees, and somehow, he looked more dignified and more serious—like a competent nurse.

Anti was talking to him gently.

"Akin, I came here to get well, and now that I am well, must I not go?"

"No, Anti. I like you so much. You've been very kind to me. If you go, who'll take care of me?"

The boy broke down and cried. He left Anti, still crying, and that woman turned a questioning eye on Bisi.

"Who's he?" asked Bisi.

"I don't know..."

"What do you mean, Anti?"

"I met him here at the hospital when I came, and he simply took to me, that's all."

Bisi could see Akin now at the other end of the Ward, going from one bed to the other, spreading comfort and good cheer wherever he went. All the patients were laughing and calling out to him to come to them. He moved about nimbly on his feet in a way which would have excited the admiration of a man who had normal sight.

"He appears to be quite happy," Bisi remarked. "And they like him very much here. D'you know how he got blind? Have you asked?"

"Ah, Bisi, why should I ask such a delicate question?"

"But if the boy was so good to you," Bisi said with irritation. "Why didn't you show some interest in his condition?"

"But Bisi, the boy is so thrilled! Why should I sadden him by prying into his blindness? He's useful to all of us, and we're so happy with him that no one ever thinks of the boy's own sufferings, and no one wants to make him unhappy by reminding him of them."

"H'm," sighed Bisi. "No one ever thinks of the boy's own troubles. We all have our own troubles. But learn a lesson from that boy. See how that boy is putting up with his own. Blinded for life, and he can't be more than twelve, yet he doesn't sit down and mope. He makes others happy by being happy himself."

Before the doctor came to discharge Anti, a tall young man in a white apron entered the Ward. He had a thermometer in his hand, and from the way the patient looked at him, Bisi knew that he was the nurse in charge of the Ward, and she sought to find out from him a little more about Akin.

"Good evening, Nurse," Madam Bisi said.

"Good evening, Madam."

He moved away to the woman who Anti had said had not allowed her to sleep on the previous night. When he had recorded her temperature and made certain notes on her progress, he came towards Anti.

"You're leaving us today." He smiled.

"Yes," said Anti.

"Well, I hope there won't be a relapse."

"No," Anti assured him. "I'm all right now. Nurse, I want to ask you something."

"Yes?"

"My friend here—Madam Bisi—would like to know a little about Akin..."

"Oh, I see." He looked rather unsteadily at Madam Bisi. "About—about his blindness?"

"Yes."

"Hmm. That was an accident he had, six years ago. But he would never have been blind if his parents had been less silly."

"How d'you mean?"

"Well, when he had his accident, there was just

the slightest chance that Doctor Simpson, our eye specialist, might have saved his sight. But his ignorant parents thought they knew better and tried to treat him themselves." He shrugged his shoulders. "You've seen for yourselves what crude drugs can do."

Madam Bisi coughed lightly.

"So," she said, "nothing more can be done for him? Nothing at all?"

The nurse shook his head. "No. It's too late, Madam Bisi."

The doctor came in a few moments later, and, after looking closely at Anti for a time, told her that she was free to leave.

The two women friends left the Ward together and got into Madam Bisi's taxi. Bisi was so overcome with emotion that she said not a word And. At George Avenue, Anti got down without saying good-bye, and when Bisi herself arrived at her home in Ajele Street, she said not a word to her neighbours.

She sat down in the darkness and thought of this boy, Akin. Blind, therefore, he was to remain a beggar all his life. Therefore, his talents were to waste. Because he was blind, he would never be able to do any good for himself and his friends, or even become a useful citizen of Africa.

To Madam Bisi it was unthinkable. She felt that Akin was not the kind of boy to remain blind and useless. She believed he had talent. All he needed was training. But where in Nigeria was there an institution catering exclusively for blind boys? Where? She thought hard.

"If I could find such a place," Bisi said to the empty room, "why, surely I would send that boy there, and let him be taught to read and write."

# 2
# THE BOYS' FOREST HOME

Early next morning, Madam Bisi called at the "Welfare Office. She was led up a series of spiral steps which made her dizzy and knocked nearly all the breath out of her.

"Oh," she panted. "Haven't we got there yet?"

"A little more," said the guide soothingly. "We'll soon be there. The Welfare Office is right at the top."

When at last they arrived at the top, it was to find that the Welfare Officer had not arrived, and Madam Bisi was shown a seat into which she gratefully lowered herself.

"Oh," she murmured wearily. "If only he can help me."

She wondered whether the Welfare officer was really the man to handle such a problem. She asked a few clerks what they knew about the education of the blind but heard nothing encouraging from them.

Mr. Marshall came in at last, and after a little delay requested that Madam Bisi be ushered into his presence. He was a medium-sized Englishman with grey eyes and a quiet manner.

"Please sit down, Madam," he said, waving her into a seat. "And what is the problem?"

"It's about a boy," began Bisi. "His name is Akin, and he is blind. I've come to find out certain things..."

"Hmm," grunted Marshall.

"You see," Bisi went on,' "I had the idea that you handle this sort of thing here, juvenile offenders, the education of bund boys, and things like that."

"Hmm...well?"

"I want to send Akin to school where he can meet other boys, especially blind ones."

Mr. Marshall smoothed the back of his neck. "Er—yes. The man you want is Fletcher. It will mean a journey out of Lagos, but if the case is as pressing as you make it, I suppose you can manage."

"I should think I can. Who's Fletcher?"

The Welfare Officer drew a case from his hip-pocket and offered a cigarette to Madam Bisi. "You don't smoke? Well, well, well! I can't talk properly without a cigarette in my mouth. Pardon me..."

He lit one, and after one or two long puffs, said, "Well, this man Fletcher...he's running an establishment which he calls the *Boys' Forest Home*. I'll tell you how it all started. He had just come out from England to do welfare work, and we were having a lot of trouble with little boys in Lagos. You know the sort I mean, thieves and the like. There was not much we could do in the way of punishing them, and this man Fletcher hit upon the idea that it would be worth his while to try to reform these African boys in a novel sort of way. So off he went into the bush with a handful of the worst of them, and they cleared a wooded area on the River Ogun.

"They put up several buildings—entirely unaided—and today you should see the Boys' Forest Home. Booming is the only word I can think of to describe it. Dormitories, dining-rooms, classroom, workshops, a gymnasium—in fact, everything necessary to keep a boy's mind off crime has been provided. I tell you Fletcher has made men out of them, and I think he's just the fellow to handle this Akin you talk about."

"But Akin is not a problem boy," said Bisi. "He's blind, and I want him educated. Are there any pro-visions for that kind of thing in the Boys' Forest Home?"

"I couldn't tell you that, Madam. You'll have to see Fletcher himself. Meantime, I'll write and tell him you're coming."

Madam Bisi thanked Marshall and left. At the foot of the spiral staircase, she bumped into a slim young woman who seemed in a hurry to get up. She was about to apologize when she heard her own name. She looked up and found herself facing Anti.

"Hello, Anti. Where are you going?"

"I've just come to collect some papers for my little boy."

"Oh, I see. I'm sorry about yesterday. I was so touched by the sight of that boy that my mind was carried miles away, and I could say nothing."

"It's all right," said Anti, and she mounted the steps and disappeared.

Bisi stood there for a moment and then went home. She did not set out for the Boy's Forest Home until the next day, and then not in a very hopeful frame of mind. It was a tiresome journey, full of enquiries after the right road.

When the taxi put her down in front of the bamboo building facing the River Ogun, Madam Bisi sighed with relief. A little boy in a white shirt showed her into Mr. Fletcher's sitting-room, and for the first time in her life, Bisi realized how attractive a bamboo house could be, if tastefully furnished. The colours had been so well chosen that the room gave her a cheerful impression of friendliness and she was almost in good spirits when the little man entered.

"Good evening, Madam," said Fletcher, "Mr. Marshall has written to me about you. Do sit down."

"This is a nice room," said Bisi, admiringly.

"Yes," admitted Fletcher. "And d'you know, the boys made all the furniture themselves! This cane chair I'm sitting in, for instance—it was woven by two little boys of ten and eleven. Oh, yes—they learn to be useful citizens here, instead of crooked ones."

He smiled, and Bisi smiled too.

"That's just the thing I want you to make of Akin, Mr. Fletcher. But his own case is different because he's blind."

"Yes," said Fletcher. He waited as if he wanted her to go on, and then, "Well, you know, the whole thing is still largely experimental. As a matter of fact, I was thinking of taking on this problem of blind boys. I've sent in an indent for equipment for the education of the blind. But you know how things are in England at the moment. It'll be some time coming out. And then, there's the problem of staff and so on, I'm hoping to get a young woman out from England... You see, Madam, there's still plenty to do."

"Hmm. But, Mr. Fletcher, won't it be possible for you to take on Akin as a private pupil of yours, and teach him to read and write?"

"Well, I could consider that. But he wouldn't learn very much. Most of my instruction will be oral. We haven't got a piano here, no relief maps for Geography and no raised Braille letters for the blind. You see, a school for the blind should furnish all these facilities. I believe in doing a thing well or not at all. When I actually get moving, I mean to include languages, mathematics, and especially music."

Mr. Fletcher had left his seat and was pacing the room excitedly. He was a small man, but his ideas seemed to have given him an added lift, and he rose in Madam Bisi's estimation. Shrugging his shoulders carelessly, he said, "Well, we must wait, that's all. We can't do these things in one day. Go back to Lagos, and send me this boy, Akin. I'll see what I can fix up for him."

Before Madam Bisi returned to Lagos, Fletcher took her on a short visit round the establishment. Some of the boys were in the gymnasium, a few more were gardening, but most of them were absorbed in their handicrafts. Everything she saw made her more anxious that Akin should come here and share this usefulness with the boys.

At the gate, Mr. Fletcher asked Bisi what she thought of it all.

"It's a good place," she concluded. "Thank you, Mr. Fletcher, and the best of luck to the Boys' Forest Home."

Mr. Fletcher's cigarette bobbed up and down between his lips. For a moment he stared at her in embarrassment.

She said, "The boy! I haven't even told him what I'm planning to do. I wonder whether he'll like the idea?"

When she got back to Lagos, Madam Bisi made all the arrangements for Akin to move over, and then she realized that one great thing remained to be done, winning Akin's confidence.

She was too tired to call at the hospital at once, but at dawn she went and spoke to the Nurse. He was in the emergency reception room, filling a card for a man whose eye had been bashed in by something or other. As soon as he had stitched the eye, he came over to Bisi.

"Hello, Madam, anybody ill again?"

"No, Nurse, I've come for something else."

"About Akin?"

"Yes. I want you to do something very important for me. I don't know him well enough, and he may be rather suspicious of my motives."

"Quite right. Make it short, you can see we're very busy."

"I have taken a fancy to him. To my mind, beating a samba is not the thing for him. He has talent, he's quite fit, only he's blind. So I thought I could train him to be useful to himself and to the country. I've already made all the arrangements."

The Nurse frowned. He was about to say something when the orderly interrupted him. He whispered a few words into the Nurse's ear and left.

"Well, Madam, I'm wanted in the operating theatre. About this boy, Akin. You don't need to worry too much. He was meant, to be a wanderer, and you can't change his spots, however you try."

"What d'you mean?"

"Well, Akin has somehow got wind of your movements, and has left. I don't know where he's gone to. If you'll excuse me," he said, hurrying away. "I must be going for that operation. Cheer up, Bisi."

He made the last remark as Madam Bisi brought out her handkerchief and pressed it to her nose, while her fat body shook with sobs.

# 3
# AKIN MEETS HERBERT

That same evening, while Madam Bisi sat in her room at Ajele Street, unable to get over her shock, Akin-was-beating his samba along a street of no great importance.

'He was alone with the trees and the birds, and his hands moved over the face of his little drum with no conscious effort of his own. Rather, it was as if those hands told his listeners of his inner unhappiness. The rebel in him was awake, and he was determined to be alone, free to follow his life in his own way.

He sat down by the roadside and gently caressed his beloved drum, murmuring a little tune to the accompaniment of the slow rhythm. If he had had eyes, he might have seen that he was in a part of Lagos slightly outside the usual tarred roads and story-houses, for here were trees and birds and grasshoppers.

But even though he couldn't see, he had wonderful ears. He knew that someone was coming up the path long before any boy with normal sight might have guessed. It was a light step, and as the owner approached, he whistled a dance tune, and sometimes sang. His voice was not yet broken. Akin guessed that it must be a boys.

He stopped beating his samba and paused to listen. The steps became louder, and a voice said,

"Hey! What are you doing there?"

"I'm resting," said Akin.

The boy came nearer. Akin could feel him peering curiously into his face.

"What happened to your eyes?"

"I had an accident and now I can't see. I am a blind boy."

"I'm sorry," said the stranger. "I'm just returning from the market. If I delay any longer, my master will be annoyed with me."

"Your master?"

"Oh yes. He's a teacher at Ilekan College, just around the corner. D'you like to come with me? My name's Herbert. When I finish cooking his supper I shall take you home. It's too dark for you to go alone."

Akin agreed to follow Herbert to Ilekan College, and that was really how he came to live there. When he got there, it was too dark for her Herbert to lead him "home"—wherever that might be—and the supper was too delicious for Akin to feel inclined to worry himself. Day after day, he grew to like his surroundings more and more. His new friends were kind to him, and he admired Herbert for his playful energy and his talkativeness.

In the evening, they sometimes went to the college orchard to play, and Herbert would collect fruits for him. Many times they went into the neighbouring woods to gather birds' eggs, but as Akin could not see, he had to be content with touching the eggs after Herbert had collected them and brought them to him.

Often they would go for firewood, and, when they had made a big heap, Herbert would tell Akin that they had saved a small amount of money from their work, and it would be useful for buying sweets on the following day.

Akin decided that he was going to like living with Herbert and the surroundings of Ilekan College. One evening, as he sat on the steps of the little room allotted to Herbert, he was beating his samba when he heard the footsteps of several boys. Presently they were dancing to his music, and their excited footwork made him beat his samba even harder. The boys shouted with glee and their numbers grew. Akin beat that drum of his until the leather began to wrinkle. He sang until his voice cracked. At last, he stopped, he begged the boys to allow him a moment's rest. They begged him to continue, but he told them he could do no more, that it was best they came back the following evening.

Every evening the boys gathered outside this teacher's house and made such a row that the poor man was often forced to come out and shout at them to stop. In a week or two, the boys had begun to look upon Akin's drumming as their ideal entertainment and relaxation. It was not surprising that his activity should come to the knowledge of the principal, but instead of getting offended about the noise and the distraction, the principal surprised the Prefects by insisting that Akin should play for the benefit of the school on one of the "social" evenings.

Akin was delighted. Herbert offered to lend him a shirt and a pair of white shorts, a red scarf and a broad-brimmed hat, but the blind boy was against the idea of putting on colours that he himself would not see. Not even the senior prefect of the school could persuade him to change his mind.

On the appointed evening, Akin appeared in his white shorts. He had polished the bells around his drum, and, as he mounted up the stage, they tinkled pleasantly. He sat down cross-legged on the floor, feeling rather nervous as the hum suddenly died down.

And then somebody introduced him.

"Mr. Chairman, gentlemen, and boys... We have with us this evening young Akin, the famous drummer and vocalist, who has volunteered to entertain us with his samba..."

"Bring him on! Bring him on!"

All was silent again. Akin placed his drum under his left armpit and slapped it three or four times. He tilted his head to one side, and his lips parted in a smile. Then he struck again, varying the intensity of his strokes, moving the drum so that the bells sang out a stirring tune.

The boys began to shuffle in their seats. They knew the song he was singing, and they joined him. That made Akin more excited, and he raised his voice and quickened his tempo. That did it. In a moment, those boys had forgotten everything about their manners. They sprang to their feet, and with agile leaping and swaying, executed the most intricate bodily movements. They abandoned themselves to Akin's music and sang till their lungs creaked.

And suddenly Akin stopped drumming. Then the boys went wild with excitement. They yelled and screamed, and implored him to continue, but he was firm. The chairman of the meeting whispered a few words into his ear, and during that interval there was a little silence.

"My dear boys, this brings us to the end of the performance by Akin. But before we bring this meeting to a close, Mr. Marshall, the Welfare Officer, would like to say a few words to you."

Akin pricked up his ears. "Mr. Marshall, the Welfare Officer"? Was that not the man whom had told him about? The man whom Bisi had gone to see the day Anti went to collect papers from the Welfare Officer. Anti had told him that this man was arranging to have him' taken to a place called the Boys' Forest Home. But listen.

"Mr. Chairman," said the Welfare Officer, "boys, ladies, and gentlemen, I thank you for inviting me to this gathering. No doubt you've all enjoyed yourselves. I have, although I could not take part in what you call the 'high-life dance, I enjoyed watching you. It was a rare treat. The boy Akin is no stranger to me. As Welfare Officer, I come across all sorts of people, and face all kinds of problems. Hem! I won't mention names, but this boy Akin has been fortunate enough to win the sympathy of a most wealthy woman. With my advice, she has decided to send him to an establishment somewhere on the river Ogun, known as the Boys' Forest Home. There Akin will learn to read and write and to do many other things under the direction of Mr. Fletcher.

"You'll all be sorry to lose him, especially as he has made you so happy here. I'm quite sure you'll join me in wishing him a prosperous time at the Boys' Forest Home. Three cheers for Akin! Hip, hip."

The meeting came to a close, and Marshall called Akin and spoke to him.

"You played really well, Akin."

"Thank you, sir."

"Well, you've heard all this talk about your going to the Boys' Forest Home and all the rest of it. I'm sure it's the best thing for you. You may not like it now, but when you grow up, you'll never regret having learnt a useful trade."

Akin had uncomfortable choking feelings in his throat. Mr. Marshall went on to tell him of arrangements they had made for him. There nothing stiff and formal. He could take his samba along with him and play it when he liked. He would be taught to use his hands, weaving baskets, sewing, making chairs, weighing things, telling the value of money by touch, and a lot of other useful little things. He talked to Akin for about half an hour, but not once did he ask the little boy what he thought of the idea.

"And why did you run away from the hospital? Bisi got there, hoping to collect you, but you were gone."

"Excuse me, sir, I don't want to learn at all."

"Hmm. It will do you good, my boy. Mr. Fletcher will be good to you. He's a man who likes little boys."

"I don't want to go, sir."

"Well, well, fancy that! Don't be upset, Akin. I'll come here to collect you tomorrow. Have a good rest and say goodbye to your friends. I should be here in the afternoon."

Mr. Marshall stroked Akin's head kindly and left. As soon as he walked away, a little hand slipped into Akin's. It was Herbert's. Akin knew its rough feel, arid the little callouses on it.

"What was he telling you?"

"He said he wants to take me to school."

"But what of this school here?"

"It is not for people like me. But I don't want to go to any school. I want to play my drum and sing. That's all. If I can get enough money to buy a little akara to eat every day, I'll be quite happy. Herbert, I'm not going to stay here anymore."

"What are you going to do?"

"I'm going away."

"Away? But where?"

"I don't know. I'm just going away. That's all."

Herbert pressed his hand a little firmly and made him a most surprising offer.

"Listen, Akin. I have three very good friends. If you-like, I can beg them to take you in, but you'll find it hard to live with them, because they are very poor. But it will only be for a short time until you find somewhere to go."

"Who are they?"

"They're from the army, and they're living in the next village to the school. Three of them."

"And you think they'll be willing to give me food and shelter until I can move on?"

"Yes, surely!"

"I'll. think of it, then. Thank you, Herbert."

"No, Akin, you're my friend. I'll do anything for you."

That night, Akin could not sleep, He lay on his back, fighting hard not to give way to the tears which throbbed in his eyes. It was nearly midnight when he heard Herbert get up. He was still wondering where the little rascal was going when he heard, "Good. He's sleeping." And then he knew that Herbert must have been peering into his face.

In fact, Herbert had peered into Akin's face, and finding his eyes closed, had concluded that the blind boy was asleep—especially as he had got no answer when, he called Akin by name. He therefore went to the door and opened it, and in came three men.

"Where is he?" asked one of them.

"Shh! Let's not shout!" whispered Herbert.

"Have you told him about it?"

"Yes."

"What did he say?"

"He said he'll think about it. I'm quite sure he'll come round. You see, Akin is somewhat self-willed, so let's give him till tomorrow." "But we need him quickly."

"I told him you were poor ex-soldiers and that you might not be able to support him for a very long time."

"What! You fool."

One of the men slapped Herbert on the face, and he began to cry. It seemed to Akin, who was listening intently, that a hand was quickly placed over Herbert's mouth. Akin lay quite still and full of fear. But he could not help overhearing every word.

"Shut up. Don't you know the boys are all sleeping? You want to wake them and let them catch us?"

"Now, listen, Herbert! As soon as he wakes, you must correct that mistake. If you don't..."

"Oh!" Groaned Herbert. "Let go of my hand. Oh! My hand. You'll break it!"

Akin heard the door open forcibly and heard the three men leave the room. After they had left, Herbert sat in the darkness and wept. Akin could not figure it out. Could it be that these men wanted to kidnap him? If so, why did they not take him at once? And all that talk about "needing" him quickly.

Needing him for what? And, by the way, what had Herbert to do with those strange men?

As Akin thought it all over, it began to dawn on him that Herbert was mixed up in something crooked. Akin asked himself, what do I really know about Herbert? Very little indeed. It's true he gave me shelter the evening I was downcast, but what else do I know? Precious little.

At this point, Akin made up his mind. It was not like him to look for trouble. The best thing would be to leave at once. Soon he heard the clear notes of the morning bell and the boys packing up their beds and water running.

He took his drum and crept away.

# 4
# AKIN AT THE EATING-HOUSE

Akin kept to the road all day. He had his samba under his arm, but he did not play it. Nobody spoke to him as he walked along, but once or twice he heard certain people making remarks about him.

"Look at that boy," said someone. "See how he moves, do you notice that he's blind?"

"Yes. He's blind, and he hasn't got a stick to guide him. How does he know his way about?"

"He must have lived here for a long time."

"I don't think so, I've never seen him here before."

Akin moved on, paying no attention to them, and then one of them made a remark which made him laugh.

"I don't think he's really blind! He's merely pretending. I think he's one of these beggars who gum their eyelids to get money out of people."

It was a fact that some dishonest boys stooped low

to such practices, but not Akin, Whose misfortune was very real and had taken place in an accident.

Akin was still feeling very hot when he paused to rest. He knew from the coolness of the spot that he must be under a tree. His fingers touched the familiar surface of a stone, and in a moment he sat down.

Taking out his drum, he began to beat it gently to himself. A song came to his lips at once, harmonizing with his present mood. As he played, he heard the sound of halting footsteps. A coin dropped at his feet and the giver hurried on. Akin took the money with thanks.

But he was not playing for money. That little drum had become a part of him, and whenever he felt happy or gloomy its rhythmic sounds brought him relief. What he did not seem to realize was that most Africans have a weakness for a well-played drum, and that the music he produced awakened in them the same emotions as it did in him.

The sound of his own drum soon lulled him to sleep, and when he awoke it was considerably cooler. He knew that there were strangers nearby, for he could hear them talking.

"This is the place. Not so, Ayike?"

"Exactly."

Women's voices. The one addressed as Ayike had something mournful in her voice, as if she had been through some great misfortune.

"They—they burnt everything down," she sobbed. "Look! Look what is left of my eating-house!"

"Don't cry, Ayike. Everything will be all right. God will provide!"

"That's what they've been telling me since last week. But where am I going to get the money to rebuild it?"

"Be patient, Ayike. If God wills it, you shall surely rise again."

"That wicked man," sobbed Ayike. "I'll never marry him, even if he burns down the very house in which I live."

"Please don't talk like that. I know what that man can do.

She broke down completely, and for the next few moments Akin could hear her friend comforting her. An idea suddenly came into his head. Suppose he offered to help her? It appeared she had met with some big misfortune. Akin himself was feeling as downcast as she was. He had no clear idea in his mind what he would do, but the very idea of offering help appealed so strongly to him that he decided to attract the women's attention.

He raised his drum into its usual place under his left armpit, and thudded at it in the craziest rhythm he knew, then he sang a song in Yoruba, about a woman who had lost everything in the world and then bad luck befell her. She lost her children, she lost her husband, she lost all her wealth, but she was not disheartened. She decided to live on, to do good to all who came her way. She never became rich again, neither did she marry, but she brought joy to many and when she died everybody in the town was very sorry to miss her.

It was a most unusual song that Akin made up on the spot, on the spur of the moment. When he had finished, the woman approached him.

"Little boy," said Ayike. "Was that a true story?"

"I don't know," said Akin. "It's just a song. It may be true, it may be false. But what does it matter?"

'No, nothing. I just wanted to know."

They stood there, undecided whether to go or to stay, and then Ayike said, "What are you doing here?"

"Resting."

"And then—where do you hope to go after that?"

"Nowhere."

The women looked at each other. "He's blind," they whispered.

"Where do you come from?" asked Ayike.

"From far away. And I'll keep on moving unless you want me to come with you."

"But your parents. Won't they object?"

"I have no parents."

"O—oh! We're sorry."

"No need to be sorry. They're not dead. They've merely thrown me out, because I'm blind, and a burden to them. But it isn't their fault. I'm of no use to them. Please don't blame them."

The women were silent. Ayike looked at this boy who had less than nothing in the world, and his calm face and plucky spirit gave her immediate courage. Her own troubles seemed to have vanished with the wind.

They sat down beside him and spoke to him gently. Gradually, Akin told them about himself. He told how a certain Englishman was trying to "educate" him, how painful it would be for him to go into the same school as normal boys who would keep reminding him of his disability, and how he had decided instead to roam the countryside.

"With this samba of mine", he concluded, "I shall always be happy."

"I'm sorry to hear all this, Akin. I would have helped you, but we were just talking about my misfortune when we heard you singing. You see that place where you are now sitting was once a thriving eating-house, until one of my customers burnt it down because I refused to marry him."

"I'm sorry. But perhaps I can help you," said Akin brightly.

"You? A little boy like you—but how?"

"Never mind! Do you cook well?"

"I think so. Most of my customers enjoy my food."

"Can you borrow a little money from your friends? Just enough to cook one day's meals?"

Ayike and her friend held a brief consultation. Then Ayike's friend said, "I think I can manage a few pounds."

"All right! I have a proposal to make. My father once told me about a certain place in England. People used to go there to eat, and, according to him, there was a man who sang to them as they ate. He attracted many people to the eating-house because of his good voice. I'll do all I can to draw crowds here with my tambourine. You can take all the money and build yourself a new eating-house. All I ask is a full stomach and a mat to lie on at night. When you have built the new place, I shall continue my journey. What do you say?"

Ayike said she was willing to do anything to put the business on its fee once more, but the other woman complained about the absence of a roof.

"Where are the people going to set?" she said.

Akin brushed aside her objections. "In the open. In the sunshine. Isn't this the dry season? By the time the rains come, there will be shelter."

"By the grace of God," said Ayike. "I think you are right."

And so, the next day, Ayike set up a grate in the open, a little distance away from the ashes of her old eating-house. Akin was beside her with his drum, and if ever he had put his very soul into his music, it was on that opening day of the new eating-house.

People who passed to work heard him singing, and they paused, then they came nearer and stood in little mystified groups watching him and listening.

"Don't you like to sit down?" Ayike would offer.

And when they had sat down, and listened to him for some time, Ayike would suggest a little refreshment, during the course of which she would tell the pathetic story of the little blind boy.

It was a formula that never failed to work. Within one-month Ayike had made sufficient money to put up a new and larger eating-house, with a large number of girls to cook, buy the ingredients and serve the customers.

One afternoon, Akin was playing for the eating-house guests. The place was packed and as he made his way from one group to another he noticed that someone was accompanying him with a guitar. Akin had an ear for music, and though the player was plucking at the strings very gently, the little blind boy readily picked him out.

He came nearer to the musician and said,

"Who are you?"

"We are musicians," said a chorus of voices. "Three of us. One of us plays a guitar, the other a bottle, and the third man has a calabash with beads. We have come here so often that we know all your songs by heart."

"And do you like them?" asked Akin.

"Yes, they're good songs. You sing of love and poverty, and truthfulness and loyalty. Everyone loves your songs. They go to the heart of every African."

Akin sighed, "You make me happy by those words."

"Yes. They're true words. We came here, hoping to try out some tunes with you. Do you like that?"

"Oh yes, which one shall we sing?"

"What about the one of the women who lost everything?"

They played the tune with such success that the patrons left their food and performed jerky little movements which few critics would have recognized as dancing.

From that day forward, the three men joined Akin, and they always played together. They readily agreed to make Akin their leader. Trade boomed for Ayike, but never once did she think of rewarding Akin for his pains, neither did Akin ask her for a penny.

The eating-house had closed down late one night, and all the waiting girls had gone home. Akin was wandering round the house, when near the kitchen the sound of harsh words reached his ears. Someone was quarrelling with Ayike.

"If you don't want that, you may go away! You came here on your own. I did not beg you to come, and I don't want you to stay. If you're not satisfied with what I've given you, go away!"

"No need to get annoyed, Madam. Since you don't want to pay us anymore, we'll go."

Those were the three musicians. Akin heard them grumble in low voices, and a door was banged. Next moment, their footsteps were sounding down the length of the empty eating-house. They were leaving. Perhaps they would never come back, these cheerful men who had kept him so happy during the past few months.

"Tayo!" he called. "Tayo, where are you going?"

"Never mind, Akin."

"Will you be coming back?"

"Never mind, Akin."

"Come back now. Please don't go!"

Akin broke into a sob and ran after them, but a table knocked him in the thigh, and when he regained his balance, he knew that the three members of his band were gone for good. He heard Ayike counting her takings for the day in a private room. He went in and listened to the greedy chink of coins.

"Madam, what have you done?" he said harshly. "Why have you sent away my friends?"

"Let them go, they are thieves and vagabonds."

"What! Thieves and vagabonds?"

"Yes, Akin. Perhaps someday when you grow up, you'll understand."

"Tell me now, Ayike. I want to understand. I am very angry with you for what you've done."

"Now, Akin, they were very bad people. They kept on obtaining money from me, and they were telling me all the time to give them more money otherwise they would carry me off my force to that man who wanted to marry me. You see, it was he who sent them to lure me away, but when they got here, they met you and were happy. So, they decided to stay, but on the condition that I was always giving them money."

Akin did not understand it. He saw Ayike only as a selfish woman who had deprived him of his music-loving friends. He spoke his mind to her.

"I'm going to leave you, Ayike. You've treated me very badly, and I shall never speak to you again."

"You don't mean that, Akin." There was fear in her voice. "What am I going to do? Akin, I beg you to stay. I'll do everything for you, my little boy. I'll buy you clothes, and a new drum, I'll get other people to play with you "

"Don't worry, Ayike. I've done my part. Did I not promise to stay with you until the new eating-house was built? Now, I have kept my promise. You have built your house and made a little money. I shall now go back to the road."

"Don't go, Akin! I beg you…come back!"

Ayike ran to him and held him, and cried and begged him, but Akin would not listen. He freed his hand from her grip and started along the road. Ayike stood there weeping loudly. She could hear the boy beating his samba and singing about a woman who was very rich and then she lost everything. Ayike remembered how Akin had sung about a woman who lost everything and never lost hope. She was afraid. Were his words ominous?

# 5
# THE VOICE OF THE ORO

Akin's departure from the eating-house brought Ayike nothing but misery. Day after day she would sit by the fireside, watching her maids prepare the food, but when it had been served out, the customers would eat it without smiling and with an air devoid of cheer. It was just as if they had merely come there hoping to meet Akin and now that he was gone they found the food tasteless and unattractive.

"Where's Akin?" a man would ask Ayike. "Where's the boy with the samba?"

"He's gone home to his mother."

"When is he coming back?"

"I don't know."

"Or have you quarreled?" the man persisted. "Ayike, you are very hot-tempered. Did you beat him?"

"Don't ask me! I don't know. He said he was going to see his mother, and he went! Was I to hold him down?"

"There now! You're losing your temper again!"

Ayike felt the hot tears clouding her eyes once more and ran quickly towards the kitchen. But she could not easily forget the picture of the little boy in the white shorts. She believed that one of these days Akin would be driven back to her if by nothing else than by hunger and poverty. But one month followed the other and she did not even meet anyone who had seen him anywhere. She began to lose hope.

It was during the Oro festival that someone dealt Ayike a cruel blow. The symbol of the Oro is a flat piece of bamboo attached to a string. When the string and bamboo are swung round the head, the flat piece of bamboo vibrates and makes a terrifying noise,

"Voo-oo! Voo-oo! Voo-oo!"

The shrill sound makes children tremble, especially when heard in the head of the night. Women are not allowed to go out at night and wander about the streets during the Oro festival. A woman venturing out could be severely beaten.

Now, since Akin left, business had been slacked for Ayike, and she began to have ideas of selling out. The eating-house. She was tidying up one night when she heard,

"Voo-oo! Voo-oo! Voo-oo!"

It was the Oro, the voice of the dog of Oro. What

was she to do? It was late—very nearly midnight. All her maids had gone home, and she was alone, and a terrible wind began to blow so that she had to shield her oil lamp by cupping her hand around the flame.

When she had finished putting the plates away, she locked up and set out alone for the bus stop, telling herself, "This is Lagos. No one will molest me. I have only to pass that dark wood in front of me and I am safe in the city. Quite safe."

She spoke to the rhythm of her footsteps, but "Voo-oo! Voo-oo! Voo-oo!" came the voice of Oro's dog. Oro was said to have a dog that howled in this terrible manner, but no one had ever seen this animal.

Ayike did not listen to it, but kept moving. She could not tell which was louder, her heartbeats or her footfalls. Her breath came in quick puffs. But she kept on moving, without throwing a glance behind her. All about her was that thick wood now, with the lurking shadows.

In the light of a weak moon, she thought she saw the mischief-makers crouching ... crouching ... waiting to spring. She started humming one of Akin's tunes, but the voice of the Oro kept butting in, and her own voice lost its cheer. Then it seemed to her that someone was following her. In fact, there was someone behind her. When she stopped, the footsteps stopped. When she looked back, she saw empty darkness. She felt like screaming at the ghostly wood. She moved faster, faster, trying to shake off the intruders.

Now she saw them. they were dressed in black, crouching as they came, their arms extended. The sounds they uttered were more like those of an animal than of a man. This was not a real incident, surely. She must be dreaming. But how did the figures overtake her and surround her?

Even in her terror, she noticed that there were three of them, wearing masks and masquerade outfits. They swung long whips above their heads.

"No! I beg, don't whip me!"

"Ha, ha!" came a cracking laugh. "Do you remember us?"

"Leave me!"

"We are the three musicians whom you sent away!"

Ayike's mouth opened with terror. These men would not spare her. She knew it. She prayed only that they should not whip her to death.

"We have been waiting for this chance," the shortest man told her, waving his rawhide whip. "Your money cannot help you now. And remember— you can do nothing about this. The Government encourages us to enjoy our festivals."

"But not to use them as a pretext for flogging your enemies!"

"Ha, ha! You wait and see!"

They tucked their whips behind their backs, and, for a moment, they stepped away and whispered among themselves. Ayike could hear her own heart beating with fright. Then one of them came back and spoke.

"Our master—the one who wants to marry you—sent us to you."

Ayike said nothing.

"Did you hear? He wants you to come with us."

"Now?" stammered Ayike.

"Yes, now."

"I cannot come. It is too late. Go and tell him I'll come tomorrow."

"He said that if you refuse to follow us willingly we should bring you to him by force. He is getting tired of begging you to be his wife."

"Oh, Lord!" gasped Ayike. "What kind of a trouble is this? Is it the custom in your place to marry by force? He has burnt down my eating-house and that is enough! What more does he want with me?"

"Don't be angry, Madam. We are doing what we've been paid for. Our master thinks you are a very beautiful woman, that's why he's doing all this."

"You cowards! Frightening a poor woman for nothing."

"Call us what you like, but we must do our duty." They sprang at her, seized her by the shoulders. She struggled to get free, but she was entirely powerless against the three stalwart musicians.

"Let me go!" she screamed. "Let me go!" The thought of going to meet that ex-soldier with his wild moustaches and rough manner terrified her, and, in a reckless moment, she tore open the mask of one of the Oro men. This was considered the greatest indignity to which any Oro man could be subjected, a man supposed to come from the other world, to have his mask stripped open by a mere woman.

The three men uttered a yell of fury. Putting Ayike down they drew those long whips and thrashed her until she was unconscious. They were lifting her limp body in their arms, not quite certain whether they had thrashed the very life out of her when they heard the sudden stampede of hooves.

They dropped the body and, as one of them tried to get away, a charging animal came out of the moonlight and hit him in the chest, and he was flung into the wood. The two others made off in opposite directions.

The owner of the animal was a cattleman. As was usual at the night-time, he was walking his bull to the slaughterhouse. He had come from a little camp a few miles away from the suburbs and his path lay through Ayike's eating house. Now, as the animal reared upon the Oro masquerader, he had the sudden impression that his bull had knocked down and killed Ayike.

"By Allah!" he cried, glancing nervously round. "What shall I do now?"

He had made up his mind to sneak away, leaving Ayike to her fate, when he heard her cry for help. She was not dead. Bending down carefully over her, he lifted her on to his shoulders and at that early hour made for the hospital.

# 6
# AKIN MEETS NURSE JOE

Akin played his drum from one village to another, until one day he stumbled upon a market at the foot of the Carter Bridge in Lagos. Though it was nearly evening, he could hear the hum of the people, and he knew that there were many of them still left in the market.

It was always a joy for him to feel the admiration of the crowd. Their happiness somehow came across to him, and, in such moments, he forgot that he was blind. In fact, there never was a time when he could clearly remember the days when he still had his sight and went to school and read and wrote. It was so long ago.

He stood in the middle of the market and beat his little samba, and the women left their tomatoes and dried fish, their vegetables and yams, and wriggled their bodies. There was something in

Akin's hoarse voice and stirring rhythms which made the woman restless.

In fact, one of them was so thrilled by the boy's music that, coming forward, she held him by the arm, and begged him to come and play for her—in her own house. She led him through a number of twists and turns, so that he had to splash into the wet drains and ram into people. Finally, he was climbing up a number of steps, and she was telling him in a low voice that they were nearly there.

She knocked at the door and said,

"Are you in, Joe? Please open."

Akin heard the sound of a door being opened and smelt the sharp smell of a man's cigarette.

"Who is this?" the man asked.

"It's a poor blind boy I picked up in the market. He plays very well. I want you to hear him. Sit down, boy."

Akin extended his hand to feel for the seat, and then he felt another—and familiar—hand placed on his.

"Who are you?" he asked, feeling its surface. "Whose hand is this? It reminds me of someone I know."

Akin had a very good memory for almost every-thing he touched. He could remember its shape, its texture, every impression it made on his fingers.

"This is the hand of an old friend," he said.

"Akin," said Nurse Joe. "What are you doing here?"

"Ah!" exclaimed Akin, recognizing the voice.

"It's the Nurse. My nurse. What are you doing here?"

Nurse Joe laughed mischievously.

"This woman is my friend. She's ill, and I've come to see her."

Akin was much too happy to listen to his explanations. "I never knew I should meet you again," he said, between sounds of pleasure. "Oh, I am so happy."

"Sit down and tell us everything."

"There is nothing to tell," said Akin. "I left you, and then went to Ilekan College, where I stayed with a boy called Herbert who gave me a bed and something to eat. I would have been very happy there, but the Welfare Officer came and said he wanted to send me to a school somewhere, so I—I ran away. Then I went on to an eating-house."

He went on to tell the Nurse of his adventures at Ayike's eating-house, how the patrons used to enjoy hearing him play, and how the three musicians joined him after a time.

"I was so used to playing with them that I was very sorry to lose them. It appeared that Ayike was not paying them very well. I think that woman is a miser. She is too fond of money."

"So you left her because of all this?"

"Yes, sir."

"Hmm," grunted the Nurse. "What a pity you were so impulsive. You might have saved her life."

"Is she dead?"

"No, but very nearly so. After you left that

place, the Oro festival came on, and your three friends took the opportunity to waylay Ayike and flog her nearly to death. In fact, I shall be very surprised if she ever recovers."

Akin was shocked. "Ah—ah!" he exclaimed. "But why?"

"Well," said Joe. "I've told you what I know."

"I didn't know they were bad people..."

"You wouldn't, Akin. It's hard to tell good people from bad people until they begin to act. Look at Madam Bisi, for instance. She's a good type."

"Please let us not talk about her."

"Why not? She is a good woman. She met you for the first time, she didn't know where you came from or who you were and look what she offered to do for you. Poor boy, it's a pity you're too young to understand..."

"I don't want to go to school," said Akin.

"You truant," Joe teased. "You're so unreasonable. Madam Bisi asks nothing in return for all this. All she wants is that you should go to the Boys' Forest Home. In England, blind people do not have to beg as we do here in Africa. They have special literature of their own and can read almost everything by touch. I've seen a Bible for the Blind. One of my patients brought it into the hospital a few years ago. Akin, how would you like to read the word of God yourself?"

Akin was silent, and for a moment Joe began to imagine that he had at last won the boy over. The blind boy's face looked attractively peaceful, as though he had merely shut his eyes and would soon open them again. He must have been a beautiful African boy before that accident. It was not difficult for Nurse Joe to understand why the boy hated the very mention of the word school. It must be, he reasoned, that the boy felt that he had lost everything worth struggling for, and his little friends would keep reminding him of his sufferings by making little innocent references to his sight. What the boy needed was someone who could understand him and, quite informally, teach him all he needed to learn in intimate companionship. The sort of basis which existed between them before Bisi came along.

"Akin," said Nurse Joe. "How would you like to come back to the hospital with me? Forget all this talk about the Boys' Forest Home and let us go back and be friends as in the old days."

Akin turned his face sharply towards the Nurse. He was breathing excitedly, as if he were trying hard to make up his mind.

"Come with me, Akin! Let us go back to the hospital. You can stay with me. Do nothing if you like. See the patients. Do you know they're all asking about you? The new ones have heard about you, and they want to know you. They want to hear you sing and play your samba."

Akin seemed to have been falling in with the idea, but he suddenly shouted,

"No. No! I'm not coming. It's a trap. I'll never go to that hospital again. Lead me back into the streets."

"Akin!"

"Take me out."

"Very well, Akin."

Quietly, without any fuss, they led him downstairs. Once more in the market, Nurse Joe spoke to him.

"I know your heart is set on being a Nurse. There's nobody else who knows this. Akin, whenever you leave your wanderings, come back to me. I'll take you. I'll do my best to make you a Nurse."

Nurse Joe was right. He had hit upon Akin's most secret wish. The blind boy looked up and a new light lit up his features.

"D'you think I—I can ever be a Nurse?"

"Yes, I think so."

This time, Akin was not nearly so happy to return to the road. Those words of Joe's had struck him to the heart. He put his samba under his armpit as he walked but did not play it. It was already very late, and after having a meal in the market stall he walked to the foot of the Carter Bridge and found a spot where he could lay down his head.

The wind from the lagoon played about his bare limbs and soothed his face. Clutched to his breast, even in his sleep, was that wonderful samba of his.

# 7
# AKIN GOES ON TOUR

Akin awoke, he left his sleeping-place and made his way from Carter Bridge to Iddo railway station. Because he was blind, the man at the gate spoke kindly to him and helped him on to a train.

When the train started, Akin began to play. At first the passengers were too interested in their friends whom they were leaving behind to pay much attention to him, but as he continued to play, he felt their admiration and heard the welcome chink of coins as they dropped into his lap. He took his samba under his armpit and toured the coaches. The passengers were all the same, he judged, civil servants going on transfer, traders carrying money to the north, mothers, and their babies. But there was one coach which contained a different set of people. They appeared to be friendly, for the moment Akin struck his drum, they shouted gleefully,

"Here he conies! Hurrah! ..."

They cheered above the noise of the roaring train, and Akin was surprised. He asked them who they were, and they told him they were boys from Ilekan College, on the way to their holidays.

"D'you remember how we used to dance round that teacher's house?"

"O-oh!" exclaimed Akin.

"Sit down, Akin. Shift, boys, and make room for him."

Akin sat tightly wedged between them, and they asked him what he had been doing. He told them all he could, and in turn asked them about the college.

"Did the Welfare Officer come to look for me after I left?"

"Yes. We saw him talking to Herbert."

"He has run away," Said the boys. "Didn't you hear?"

"No," said Akin.

"Oh, well. He brought three men to burgle his master, and when that teacher tried to resist, they killed him. And, worst of all, they found nothing."

"You mean—you mean...that teacher is dead?"

"Yes. He died long ago."

Akin was silent. The train roared on. Now and again the cheer of a crowd told him that they had passed another railway station.

"He was such a good man," Akin commented.

"Why should anyone want to kill him? And why did Herbert run away?"

"We don't know, Akin. Nobody knows. The police are out looking for Herbert and three men. So, if you come across them, remember."

Akin was dazed by what he heard. However, he said, "I shall do my best to bring them to justice — if luck brings them my way."

"Now," said one of the boys. "Don't look so sad, Akin! Give us some music. What's past is past."

Akin was not in the mood to oblige, but he said cheerfully, "What d'you want me to play for you?"

"Now, let me see... What about the story of the woman who lost everything she had... remember?"

Oh, yes.

Akin started to play without interest, but their response was so warm, especially after he had bought them some bananas out of his earnings, that he began to brighten up, and in a short while he regained his usual happy mood.

He spent the rest of the time with them until they all got down at Oshogbo, where they parted, their lorries going in opposite directions. Akin travelled east, touching the important towns. At Ilesha he spent well over a week playing from one street to the other, and receiving more presents than he could conveniently carry. Then he went to Akure and Benin. He bought a strong coat and sewed the money into the lining, hoping someday to donate it to the Boys' Forest Home. He reckoned that if he did not go there himself, he could at least help Fletcher with the good work.

Wherever he went, two things struck him. One was that people had somehow learnt that he was touring the towns and were prepared and even anxious to welcome him, the other—and perhaps more shocking—was that everybody seemed to be on the look-out for Herbert, the accomplice.

# 8

# MR. FLETCHER GOES ON TOUR

Not long after Madam Bisi had left the Boys' Forest Home, Mr. Fletcher received his equipment for the education of the blind. There were all sorts of books written in Braille, models of various weights and measures, maps, diagrams, all the apparatus being addressed to the touch.

"Well," sighed the little man, rubbing his hands contentedly. "This is just the thing we want ... the very thing we want."

He buried himself in the work of sorting, cataloguing, separating and classifying all he had received. At the end of a week he had reduced his consignment into something like order, and then a new thought came to him.

Where were his pupils to come from? Surely, he would never get them by spending the rest of his life in the Boys' Forest Home. The place was far too remote and unknown to attract anyone, particularly a blind man.

He discussed the matter with Mr. Marshall, and they decided that a propaganda tour would be the right thing. So, borrowing a dozen odd films, a microphone, and two or three linguists in the African idiom, Fletcher set out on his tour. Now, while he was travelling from west to east, Akin was travelling from east to west.

Wherever Mr. Fletcher went, he told the people that Africans had got the idea that if a man was blind his potentialities as a useful citizen were reduced to zero and he had to remain a beggar all his life. That was not the case. If a man was blind, he could do many things that a man with sight could not do, because a blind man's touch was more tender than that of a normal-sighted man. He showed films to parents of the blind and invited them to talk to him about their children.

One morning, his car drew up in the town of Ile-Ife. He hired a schoolroom and went over his subject as usual, a film show, a talk, and an invitation for questions. Someone got up and said,

"We've heard all you said about the education of the blind. But what have you done about the more obvious cases?"

Mr. Fletcher looked round to see a young man in an English-tailored suit, his hands stuck in his pockets, his head cocked to one side. He looked like a schoolteacher surveying his class triumphantly.

"Obvious cases?" Fletcher echoed. "What do you mean,

"If you're to start a section for the blind in your Forest Home, why not begin with young boys of talent? People like Akin, for instance. Such boys could learn a lot now that would make them independent in the future."

Mr. Fletcher gave a guilty start.

"Did I hear you say Akin?"

"Oh, yes," said the teacher. "The boy has been in this town for about a week now. Many of us went to see him play his drum. I must say, I was very sorry to see him. Just imagine having a son of that age, and then knowing that he has no other prospects..."

"Hmm. As a matter of fact, Akin has already been enrolled in the school. He was to have reported for work some time ago, but I don't know what happened."

The teacher sat down, but he did not seem quite satisfied. Fletcher was very excited. In Ile-Ife? That was the most exciting piece of news he had heard for weeks.

After the close of the meeting, he made a thorough search of the town, but could find no trace of Akin.

# 9
# THE THREE MUSICIANS

Akin did not know anything about the visit of Mr. Fletcher until that gentleman had left for the next village. When the little boy left Ile-Ife, Mr. Fletcher was already miles ahead of him. There was no possibility of their ever meeting.

Akin was making his way on foot along the highway when he suddenly heard loud footsteps behind him. He knew that someone was following him, and he tried to hurry. There was a lot of money in his pockets, and it wouldn't do for him to lose it. He had to get back to Lagos as early as he could.

Presently, his followers caught up with him, and, as they did so, he heard a guitar, accompanied by a bottle and a gourd, all playing a tune which he knew only too well, the story of the woman who lost everything. Without waiting to find out who it was, he put his samba in position and joined them. He was wild with joy. He beat his little drum as he had never beat it before. The men took the chorus, shuffling their feet to the rhythm of the tune.

"Ha, ha, ha, Akin! We've met at last."

"Where are you people going?" asked Akin.

"We have come to join you. Where you are going, there will go, as well."

"Really?"

"Yes."

"I see," murmured Akin.

"You don't sound very pleased to see us."

"I am glad," said Akin, recalling a lot of things.

There was that night when Herbert had admitted them into his room, thinking that he was asleep. One of them had been saying something about "needing" him. Then there was this new story about the murder of the teacher at Ilekan College. Could they have been responsible for that?

"If you don't want us to follow you, we'll go away. After all, nobody has any proof that we murdered the teacher at Ilekan College."

Akin was shocked. He said, "Who talked of murder?"

"Then why do you look so serious, as if you are the one to judge us?"

Akin saw at once that it would not do to offend any of them, especially after hearing what they had done to Ayike at the eating-house. It needed some tact to handle them.

"Stay with me," he said. "Let's go to the shade. The sun is too hot."

"Very good," they said.

They led him by the hand for a short distance, and he sat down. He asked them how they had come to trace him out and they told a story of how discontented they had been since they had left the eating-house. Not one of them mentioned the incident with Ayike. While the story was going on, Akin thought he could hear a strange voice whispering to one of the men.

"Is there anybody else with you?" he asked.

"You have a wonderful ear, Akin. Yes, Herbert is here with us."

They were complete, Akin thought, the murderers, and the accomplice. This was the tightest corner he had ever been in. To be the bandleader of a crowd of murderers. If he had his sight, he would know when the police were near and hand them over. If they had been in Lagos, he might have had an idea where they were, and appealed for help. As it was, there was nothing he could do but submit entirely to their will until he had the opportunity to expose them.

"The first thing," said their speaker, "is that we want money. It's no use telling us you have none because we're going to search you."

They stripped Akin of his jumper. He heard them laughing and struggling over the contents, and then, "Phew!" whistled one of them. "This boy has money."

"One hundred pounds, ten shillings and eight pence ha penny."

Akin's throat was dry. He had no idea that he had saved up so much money. He had been in the habit of converting all his shillings into notes as soon as they were up to twenty. He had a deep pocket in the lining of his jumper, and inside this he put all his money. No thief ever thought him worthy of his attention. Akin's plan to give that money to Mr. Fletcher for the Boys' Forest Home was thus foiled in advance.

The men told him that they were going to stay by him while he made all the money. "Do not try any-thing clever, like trying to reveal us to the police. If you do, we'll kill you. And remember, you're blind. You can't run away. We'll see you and catch you. D'you hear?"

Akin broke down. He sobbed, and when he wouldn't stop, the men started to beat him up. He told them they were just being wicked, that he had done nothing to them, and still they beat him up.

After that, they went from one town to the other, playing only at night. They never failed to raise both money and admiration. Akin was becoming a national character, loved by his people, able to stir the deepest emotions within them, and so harmless that everyone gave—and gave freely—whenever he played. And behind him hung that shadow of Herbert and the murderers.

Shortly after this, something happened which ended the partnership, but before then a chief had invited Akin to play for him and, reckless as they were, Herbert and the three musicians had agreed to take part in the show.

62

# 10
# WHEN THE SAMBA SPOKE

The time drew near when Akin would play for the chief, but he did not feel happy. If only he could get the three musicians to keep out of it, things would look better, but the three men refused to agree with him. They argued that he knew too much about them, and it would be unwise to let him out of their sight. Moreover, they had made up their minds that this would be their last partnership together. With their takings at this show, they reckoned that they would have enough to live on for some time.

The day before they were to make their public appearance, the musicians decided to take Akin for a short walk—by way of publicity, they explained.

They set out in the evening and walked slowly. Most of the people whom they passed paid no attention to them probably because Akin was not playing his samba. It was a fairly big town, about thirty miles from Lagos. A lot of people rode in cars, and the streets were lit with electric light.

When they had walked for about an hour, they told Akin to sit down and rest. "This is the' place," said one of them. "We can sit here and play, and anyone who sees us will ask what we're doing, and then they'll get to know about the show."

"Is this not the road to the hospital?" asked Herbert. "Yes, it is. And there is the soldiers' barracks behind us. A lot of people will pass this way."

Akin did not feel at all pleased, but it was good to be out again in the open. He brought out his samba and, as he usually did when he was in a bad mood, he played it gently. His songs had a weird theme in them this evening. He sang of death, of the death of a certain teacher whom the thieves supposed to be rich, and when they had killed him, they found that he had nothing.

A man tapped him on the shoulder and said, "Boy, do you mean what you're saying? Do you really know the people who killed the teacher? Have no fear. Tell me, I am a policeman. There is a reward of one hundred pounds for the man who will give us information leading to the discovery of the rogues..."

Akin repeated his song, and the policeman said, "Yes. But where are they? You say they're beside you?"

While the policeman was arguing with Akin, Herbert and the three musicians met a short distance from the crowd and went on to the real business which had brought them to the barracks.

"This is the place," said Herbert.

"OK! You stay here, Herbert. We will go inside. If you see anyone coming, whistle gently, like this..." he imitated an owl's hoot.

"I understand," said Herbert. "You've got your tools, I hope?"

"Yes, where is the bag? Good. We go!"

The three musicians rolled up the sleeves of their colourful gowns, and, leaving the gourd, the bottle, and the guitar in Herbert's care, slipped through the barbed-wire fence. Herbert dug himself in well enough not to be seen by the soldier on guard or anyone passing by on the main road, but well enough for his keen eyes to take in everything that went on all around him.

Then a car stopped a short distance away, and a man shone a red light three times. Herbert knew what that meant. It was their pre-arranged signal. The man who was so anxious to buy the military tires had arrived. Herbert whistled to the three musicians to hurry up, and when he looked up at the road again, a woman was coming towards him. It annoyed him to know that he had given away his position by such a simple act. "Herbert," said the woman when she came near. "What are you doing here?"

"I—I" stammered Herbert.

"Remember me?" she said. "I am Ayike of the eating-house. I've just come out of the hospital, and

I'm living here in the barracks with my new husband. You little rascal! Still playing your pranks?"

Herbert said nothing.

"Won't you come along with me? Your friend Akin is playing down there. Let's go and see him."

"N-no, Madam. I—I..."

The man in the long coat came nearer.

"I hear," said Ayike, "that your master is dead. You did not really arrange for those thieves, did you? I know you didn't. Many people thought you knew something about it because you ran away."

Herbert made a noise of some sort, and Ayike said, "Eh? What did you say?"

The man in the long coat interrupted them.

"Herbert?"

"Yes, sir."

"Good. Where are the tires?" He dug his hands impatiently into his long robe and growled, "If you deceive me this time, I'll give you up!"

"Please, sir..."

The business man turned to Ayike. "What is she doing here?"

The Ayike understood. With one swift movement, she darted away, while Herbert shouted,

"Hold her!"

It was too late. Ayike was already down the road. She was shouting at the top of her voice that she had seen Herbert, the accomplice, that he was stealing tires a short distance away.

Cries of "Thief! Thief!" filled the air.

Where he sat playing his samba, Akin heard

these alarms, but he did not understand what was going on.

When he stood up, he heard a man shout, "There he is! The small boy, there he is! Hold him!"

Confused, and a little terrified, Akin decided to stand where he was. Then someone ran past him, shouting wildly to him to run "for his life". It was Herbert, but why was he running? What had gone wrong? Why was his voice so full of terror? Akin began to move. He remembered how often an innocent man could be mistaken for the guilty. He did not want to wait for bad luck to overtake him.

He quickened his pace.

"Stop!" cried a voice behind him. "Stop, there! D'you hear me? If you don't stop, I shall shoot! By Allah! I shall shoot. Take this!"

A shot rang out.

"Oh!" groaned the blind boy. "Oh! I'm dead. They've killed me!"

He fell in a heap.

The soldier came up to the fallen boy.

"Get up! If you'd run another step, I'd have shot to kill."

So I'm still alive! thought Akin. "I—I'm not a thief, only a beggar..."

The soldier looked into Akin's eyes and immediately saw his mistake. He helped Akin to his feet. Just then, another shot rang out.

The soldier looked up and saw a woman coming up the path.

"Akin ... are you all right?"

It was Ayike.

"Yes, Ma. They nearly killed me."

"I only fired a warning shot," explained the soldier. "But the shock got him down, or perhaps he tripped."

"I tripped and fell," cried Akin. "My ankle is burning.

"Never mind, Akin," Ayike said in a soothing voice. "After this, I don't think your friend Herbert will ever steal again."

A group of soldiers carrying rifles came up. Behind them, two soldiers came carrying a stretcher.

"They stripped two tires," said the leader of the group. "They were working on the biggest one when we saw them. We shot this one in the leg. The other escaped."

The man on the stretcher began to moan, and Akin in his terror recognized the voice, one of the musicians of the eating-house.

One of the soldiers put something down and it fell with a chink. "We collected their tools, a guitar, a gourd and a bottle."

"O—oh!" exclaimed Ayike, suddenly seeing the light. "So, Herbert brought the three musicians to come here and steal tires. Aha! And he was their watchman. Clever boy! So while Akin played his samba, the thieves were at work. Oh!"

She looked at the man on the stretcher, one of those who had maltreated her on the night of the Oro. "I must see that you're all well repaid," she murmured.

# 11

# NEW NAMES ON FLETCHER'S REGISTER

Ayike did not find it easy to catch Herbert and the two musicians. She found, on her arrival in Lagos, that Madam Bisi was availing enough to help with all the money at her command, while Nurse Joe kept a careful check on all the patients who came into the hospital and told his friends in the other hospitals to be on the lookout for the other two men and Herbert. But for three months, it seemed as if the culprits would get away with their crimes.

Then, one afternoon, Ayike saw a man being followed down the road by a rough and angry crowd. He was carrying a mud image on his head, and the villagers were slapping him right and left, very freely.

"Thief!" they shouted.

Ayike was amused by the way the feeblest members of the crowd availed themselves of this opportunity to maltreat the big man. The women and children seemed to be most anxious to slap him and throw sand in his face. His face, wait... That face was a familiar one. There it was, the face of one of the wanted men, Ayike was certain. A musician. She felt all hot inside. She remembered the night when this same man had flogged her with a whip.

What was she to do? She was twenty miles out of Lagos, a woman, unarmed, and not strong enough to knock him out and take him in by sheer force.

"I'll see if there's a police station here. I've often seen policemen here—"

She made enquiries and was directed along a narrow lane. The Constable on duty knew her. He had often made eyes at her when she came there to buy plantains. That was bad, because at first he did not take her word seriously. But soon the angry cries reached him, and he took the phone and rang up headquarters.

The one or two hours of waiting that followed were the longest in Ayike's life. She stood at a corner of the charge office, and the angry mob brought the musician up and charged him with violating their god. The policeman took down notes, and asked the prisoner whether he had ever been convicted before.

Time dragged heavily on. The policeman was up to his neck in work, sifting reports and counter-reports, false statements, repetitions and contradictions. At last, Ayike heard the drone of the police car. She had won!

Policemen jumped out of the kit-car. What method they used to make, the big musician reveal the hideout of Herbert and of the other musician Ayike could not tell, but when she was called upon to identify Herbert and the other man late that same evening, she could not help admiring the cleverness of the police.

The trial that followed was not a long one. Ayike was surprised but not in the least bit sorry for the biggest of the musicians when he started crying in the witness-box. He confessed that Herbert had been the "contact" and the "brains" of the gang. This little boy, not more than twelve years old, had had a bad record. Sent out of school for substituting someone to take the entrance exam for him, he had gone on to forgery, burglary and arson. It was he who, paid by the ex-soldier who loved and lost Ayike, had burnt down the first eating-house. He had been in close touch with the three musicians all along and had suggested using the blind boy Akin as a "cover" for all their future crimes.

The musicians admitted having murdered the teacher but pleaded for leniency. It was all a mistake, they said. They had made up their minds to break away from Akin after the show for the chief, but Herbert had seen a man who was ready to pay a lot of money for the tires and had suggested using Akin again as "cover" for their theft.

Ayike sat in the court and wondered whether to feel sorry for the two musicians, and especially for the one who had been shot in the thigh. She felt the tears coming to her eyes when she thought of the punishment that awaited them, but then she remembered how they had treated her and what crimes they had led the innocent Akin to commit, and she braced herself to hear the judge's sentence.

When she heard the actual words of the judge, committing the three musicians to be hanged by the neck until they were dead, she fainted away.

She was still unconscious when Herbert's sentence was pronounced, so she didn't know that until later.

That was when she called at the Boys' Forest Home. Bisi and Nurse Joe were with her, and after talking generally for some time, Fletcher announced that he had gained two pupils, a good one and a bad one. He took them to the Carpentry Shed, where a boy in shorts was very busily making a box out of cheap wood. The boy looked up when Fletcher approached, and Ayike nearly fainted with shock.

"Herbert!" she cried.

Ayike caught Herbert's thievish eyes and, walking straight across, she seized a plank and bashed him on the head. He screamed, and she beat him harder, until Fletcher tore her away.

"Please, Madam, you—you can't!"

Ayike flung the plank at Herbert, and asked, "Is this all the punishment he was given?"

"No, he had six strokes of the cane every day for seven days. Then I begged that he should be brought here. Of course, if I fail to reform him, well. "He shrugged.

"Now, let's get out of here," suggested Joe.

"Yes," said Bisi, "I can't bear to look at that little horror."

"Wait," said Ayike. "We've seen the bad pupil. Where's the good one?"

"Just come with me. We'll soon find him."

While Fletcher took them round the establishment, they tried to divert themselves with more cheerful conversation. Ayike spoke about her new eating-house, and Nurse Joe talked about the hospital, and what good it was doing for the people.

"But not as much as the Boys' Forest Home will do for our blind. If only we can make them know that a blind man need not be a beggar all his life."

There was a little silence, and Madam Bisi said, "I remember when I first came to see Mr. Fletcher."

"Yes," said Fletcher. "You were so anxious to get Akin into the Boys' Forest Home."

"And now that it's happened, I hope he'll make a good pupil in his new home."

"You've let the cat out of the bag!" Fletcher exclaimed. "You've spoilt my surprise!"

"Ah!" cried Ayike. "So, Akin is the good pupil you spoke about? I'm so glad."

"Please keep the boy away from Nigeria's number one criminal. I mean, Herbert," Ayike explained.

"That's the snag," Fletcher said quietly. "The Boys' Forest Home is a kind of reformatory, you see. The Blind Section is so small at this moment that it can't yet be run separately. But we'll keep an eye on the bad ones, you bet!"

"And good luck to you," said Ayike. She looked meaningfully at Madam Bisi. "Are you going to tell him your secret? I mean about "

"Shall I?"

"Of course!"

"Well," began Madam Bisi with a sideways glance at Ayike. Then she looked at Joe and said,

"We are planning to bring Akin's father and mother here to see him. We'll pay their fare and bring them here, just to make them know their boy is alive and in safe hands."

"I think that's a good idea. They'll be very welcome. By all means bring them. I hope it'll make them change their minds towards the lad."

Just then, they heard the sound of drumming coming from the woods.

They went over, all of them—Bisi, Ayike, Nurse Joe and Fletcher. They stood a good distance away, so as not to attract the drummer's attention.

Akin wore a dark blue juniper that came down to his knees. His feet were bare and his long bony hands-held the tambourine, the samba, not in the usual manner under his armpit. He had the samba in the palms of his two hands, and his elbows were raised high above his head, and he was beating the samba in the air and the bells were jingling and his feet were tapping. The boys, the delinquents, the dangerous criminals, the thieves, the liars, the run-aways-from-home, they all crowded around him like rats around the Pied Piper. And they danced and sweated.

And just at that moment, as if even Nature herself had been conquered, the evening sun came out in one last red glow. The entire sky was transformed into a dazzling arc of red so that the white clouds were tinged, and they stood out against the red-blue sky. The trees stood out dark and silent, and all Nature seemed to focus its last effort in that red glow of Nigerian sunset.

Madam Bisi and Joe held hands. Ayike looked on, like a child lost in wonder. Akin had brought with him some form of magic, some strange enchantment and power, over Fletcher's Forest Home. She glanced at Fletcher. His eyes were misty. Bisi, too, was trying to conceal a tear, big and bold, that was quickly stealing down her cheek. She looked quickly away to the woods, where Akin the Drummer Boy was radiating happiness, in a manner to make everyone think only of doing good, and of being good, and of living a clean life.

"God bless Akin," she murmured.

And everyone around her echoed her words. Slowly they all turned, stealing back to the gate where their taxi awaited them, moving silently so that Akin would never know that they had seen him and were praying for his success.

# ABOUT THE AUTHOR

**Cyprian Ekwensi** was born in Nigeria in 1921, the son of a famed storyteller and elephant hunter. In early life, he worked as a forestry officer in Nigeria and as a pharmacist in Romford, Essex. On returning home, he wrote his first novel, *People of the City* (1954), which was one of the first Nigerian novels to be published internationally. *Jagua Nana*, his most famous book, appeared in 1961 and won the Dag Hammarskjöld prize in literature, though it was banned in schools and attacked by the church. Later in life, Ekwensi worked in broadcasting, politics, and as a pharmacist, while writing over forty books and scripts. He died in 2007. His works continue to appeal to readers all over the world.

# OTHER BOOKS BY CYPRIAN EKWENSI

*People of the City*
*The Passport of Mallam Ilia*
*King for Ever!*
*Jagua Nana*
*Burning Grass*
*An African Night's Entertainment*
*Beautiful Feathers*
*Survive the Peace*
*Masquerade Time*
*Restless City and Christmas Gold*
*Glittering City*